Books by Matt Christopher

Sports Stories

Animal Stories

The Pigeon with the Tennis Elbow

The Pigeon with the Tennis Elbow

by

Matt Christopher

Illustrated by Larry Johnson

Little, Brown and Company

BOSTON   TORONTO

FIRST EDITION

T 09/75

Library of Congress Cataloging in Publication Data

Christopher, Matthew F.
  The pigeon with the tennis elbow.

  SUMMARY: Kevin O'Toole, playing in a tennis tourna-ment, meets a talking pigeon who turns out to be his great uncle and gives him tennis tips.
  [1. Tennis—Fiction] I. Johnson, Larry, 1949-
II. Title.
PZ7.C458Pi   [Fic]   75-19468
ISBN 0-316-13966-1

Published simultaneously in Canada
by Little, Brown & Company (Canada) Limited

PRINTED IN THE UNITED STATES OF AMERICA

To John G. Keller

The Pigeon with the Tennis Elbow

THE BALL BLURRED for an instant as it boomed from Rusty Maxwell's high-swinging racket and came slicing across the net. It struck the asphalt court near the right baseline, bounced up and took a little sidewise twist.

The serve was a good one. Kevin O'Toole grimaced as he prepared to return the shot. Rusty's best play was his serve, and it had put him ahead in this game as it had in so many others.

Whoom! Kevin met the ball with a solid forehand swing, holding the racket with both hands, and sent it streaking back over the net.

His return brought a hint of a smile to Kevin's lips. The ball was heading far to Rusty's left side and Rusty was running after it full tilt.

He failed to get to it and the ball bounced past him for a tied score, 15–15.

A smattering of applause, and the cheer of a familiar voice, followed, embarrassing Kevin so that his face grew flushed.

He shot his sister a dirty look. "Oh, cut that out, will ya, Gin?" he said, though hardly loud enough for her to hear him.

Ginnie, a year younger than he, flashed dark eyes at him and gave her black hair a shake that left the long waves dangling over her shoulders. Although almost a head shorter than he, Ginnie could swing a racket with the best of them. Often she beat her brother by margins he was ashamed to talk about.

A dry laugh rumbled from a boy sitting on the bottom row of seats flanking one side of the court, and once again Kevin felt his face grow pink. Roger Murphy, a skilled tennis player and Rusty Maxwell's friend, had a knack for bugging opponents without saying a word.

Kevin took his eyes off Roger and looked over the small crowd that had come to watch the game. Ordinarily he hated being watched as he played. But, he realized, a crowd of some sort always gathered to watch a good tennis match.

He looked across the net and saw Rusty ready to serve. Spreading his legs and grabbing hold of the racket's long smooth handle with both hands, Kevin waited.

Up went the ball, and up on his tiptoes went Rusty. He met the ball squarely, driving it like a shot toward the net. It was too low, though, striking the top of the net and dropping on his side.

He tossed up the other ball that he had, rising again on his tiptoes as he offered the serve. This time the blow was softer. Kevin followed it easily and banged it back across the net, aiming it toward Rusty's left corner. Rusty got there in time and hit it back. Kevin, waiting near the back court, ran in and struck the ball hard on the peak of its bounce and sent it like a bullet toward Rusty's right corner. The shot was good and Kevin went into the lead, 15–30.

Again came the smattering of applause which Kevin pretended to ignore. He'd just have to talk with Ginnie after the game, that's all there was to it.

An out of bounds serve, then a driving serve that hit the net, scored another point for Kevin, making it 15–40, his favor.

He stepped back into the corner, taking a deep breath of the warm June air that carried with it the smell of pines from the nearby woods.

Rusty's next serve was good, and for a while he and Kevin knocked the ball back and forth, neither getting a good shot.

Then Kevin made a return from the throat of his racket. He groaned as the ball went askew toward the side of the court, striking the net and dropping on his side. 30–40.

He scored the next point, winning the game,

as Rusty belted the ball outside the right base-line. He was now leading two games to one in the first set.

He walked off the court, wiping his sweating face with a handkerchief.

"Quit making all the noise, will you?" he said in a low voice to Ginnie.

"What noise?" she said.

"You know what noise," he answered.

"You mean my cheering for you? What's wrong with that?"

"Nothing, except that you're the only one I hear. Just calm it down a little. O.K.?"

She shrugged. "O.K. But beat him, will you? I want you to play that Roger codger next."

He looked at her, then took a swallow of water from the fountain and returned to the court. Why did she have to remind him of that, anyway?

Rusty broke Kevin's serve and won the next game, making it two games apiece.

Kevin clamped his lips tightly in disgust as he heard the crowd applaud for Rusty. He had played badly in that game, and he blamed it on Ginnie. She had reminded him that the winner of today's match would play Roger Murphy, and Roger's name had stuck in his mind like a scary movie. Few guys had the ability to knock off Roger on the tennis court, and Kevin was not one of them. At least not yet. Why did she have to open up her mouth, anyway?

He tried to push Roger out of his mind as the next game started, and managed to buzz ahead of Rusty, love–30, before Rusty seemed to know what was happening. Then Rusty scored on a blistering hot serve that Kevin missed by a foot. 15–30. Kevin took the next two points, though, and won the game.

"Three more to go and it's your set," said Ginnie as he came and sat down on the bench beside her.

"Three more is a lot," he said. "I wish it was just one more."

"Oh, Kev," said Ginnie, her hands squeezed tightly on her lap. "That's your trouble. A de-featist attitude."

7

"Oh. That what it is?"

He knew that that's what it was, too. But he could not admit it. Especially to her.

Coo-coo! Coo-coo!

The sound barely registered with Kevin as he thought about going back on the court to start the next game. Then it came again, and this time he looked for its source.

He saw it, a grayish-white pigeon that was perched on top of the pole in the southwest corner of the court. Its broad wings spread out, and for a moment Kevin thought that it was going to fly off. Then it closed its wings about its round, plump body and relaxed as if it had come to watch and enjoy the game.

Coo-coo! Coo-coo! it chanted again.

"Even that pigeon is laughing at me," Kevin murmured.

Ginnie giggled. "You're a dilly," she said.

"O.K., boys!" said Ben Switzer, the playground director. "Let's go!"

Kevin got two balls from the ball boy, for now it was his turn to serve. He stood in position, tossed up a ball and rose to meet it on his tiptoes, his racket held high. Bang! The ball blazed across the net like a shot.

Rusty met it with the face of his racket, driving it back. As it struck the court and bounced up, Kevin lashed at it with a hard, two-handed stroke. Racket met ball squarely and sent it buzzing back.

Oh, no! Kevin almost screamed as he saw the ball streak for the top of the net.

It hit the net and dropped softly on the other side.

"Darn!" Rusty yelled.

There was a brief applause, then silence. A moment later the silence cracked as a voice said, "What a cheap shot *that* was."

The remark made Kevin angry. He turned and stared at Roger. Someday he'd show that wise guy!

2

KEVIN TOOK THE NEXT two points, making the score 40–love, and prepared for what could be his last serve of the game. It was a solid drive to Rusty's left side.

Rusty shifted his racket and dealt the ball a hard, backhand blow. The return was good. The ball barely cleared the net and bounced close to Kevin's right sideline. Then, even as Kevin hit the return, he knew the shot was a bad one. The ball sliced off to the left, curving outside the baseline. A point for Rusty.

Saved you from a skunking! Kevin thought.

That was the only point Rusty scored, though, and the game went to Kevin. He finished off nicely in the next two games, winning the set, 6–2.

"Well, that's one set for you," said Ginnie as Kevin plunked himself down beside her. "And you'll take the next one. You've got to."

"Oh, sure," said Kevin dismally.

"There you go. That defeatist attitude again," said Ginnie coldly. "Can't you be *positive* for a change?"

"O.K., O.K. I'm positive. All right?"

He didn't know why he did it, but at that moment he glanced over to the pole where the pigeon was resting and saw it jerking its head first one way and then the other as it seemed to peer at him out of one eye and then out of the other.

What a pet he'd make, Kevin thought. He had never had a pet, not a dog or a cat or a gerbil, or even a turtle. Neither his mother nor his father cared for animals around the house. As for Ginnie, she was on the go so much she'd never have time to spend with an animal, anyway.

Stare at me, will you? Kevin thought. *I ought*

11

*to knock you off that pole with a tennis ball,
you feathered nut.*

Kevin laughed to himself, and Ginnie nudged
him. "What's funny?" she asked.

"What?" he said. "Oh — nothing."

"Honest," she said, "you *are* a dilly."

"O.K.!" Ben Switzer yelled. "Ready for the
second set!"

It was Rusty's serve. He took the first two
games, then lost the next two. Kevin, feeling
that Lady Luck was with him, won three more
in a row. Rusty rallied and copped the next two
games. 4–5, Kevin's favor.

Kevin went to the bench and sat there until
the last second when Ben Switzer yelled, "Come
on, Kev! Let's go!" and got him to his feet.
Kevin saw that Ginnie had her fingers and ankles crossed, and her eyes closed.

Hope that silly stuff works, he thought.

His heart pounded like a drum as the ball
boy handed him the two required tennis balls.
Ginnie was right, he thought. He *had* to win.
If he lost this game, it would mean that he'd

have to play at least two more. The way he felt he'd be worthless in both, and Rusty would come out the winner.

"Ready?" he said.

"Ready," Rusty replied.

Taking a deep breath, then expelling it, Kevin tossed up one of the balls, rose on his tiptoes and gave the fuzz-covered sphere a belt that drove it across the net directly at Rusty. Rusty ducked, a smile coming over his face as he yelled, "Fault!" even before the ball hit beyond the baseline.

Kevin made the next serve good. Rusty returned it, hitting the ball gently, carefully. The ball dropped softly over the net and Kevin, running in fast, slammed the ball back into Rusty's forecourt with such force that Rusty couldn't get near it. 15–love.

After that Kevin could see that his getting the first point had taken the wind out of Rusty's sails. He won the game easily, the set, 6–4, and the match.

"Congrats, brother!" Ginnie cried, running

across the court and throwing her arms around him. "I *knew* you'd do it!"

"I suppose it was because you crossed your fingers and ankles," said Kevin as he pushed her hands off him.

"And shut my eyes," she added, her eyes sparkling. "Nice game, Rusty," she said as Rusty came forward, hand extended to Kevin.

"Don't kid me, Gin," he said. "I was lousy. Good game, Kev."

"Thanks, Rusty."

"Well . . ." Rusty sighed. "It was either you or I against Roger on Friday. I've never beat him yet. Have you?"

"A couple of times . . . last year," Ginnie answered quickly for her brother. She began dragging him away as she chattered on, smothering whatever it was Rusty was going to say. "Good luck in your next game, Rusty! You are improving a great deal! You really are! That serve could be a real ace if you could develop it a little more!"

Kevin stared at her as he let her drag him off the court and to the street.

"Ginnie! When did I ever beat Roger?" he asked, jerking his sleeve loose from her hold.

"O.K., I lied," she said, her voice an octave lower.

"Lied? I guess you did!"

"Oh, don't say it as if I had just robbed the New Laswell Bank," she blurted. "I wasn't far wrong. You were close to beating him *twice*."

"But still — that's not winning!"

A chuckle that sounded like a horse laugh came from behind them, and Kevin looked around to see who it was. The closest people were a foursome some thirty feet behind them. But they each seemed to be engrossed in their own business.

Kevin turned to his sister, frowning. "Did you hear somebody laugh?"

"Yes," she said, looking over her shoulder. "It must have been one of those characters behind us. What's the difference?"

She started to talk about Friday's tennis match with Roger Murphy, but most of what she said filtered through Kevin's brain like water through a net.

Then a flutter of wings sounded very close to his head, and he ducked. He looked up and saw a pigeon zooming upward in a wide loop. Then it glided down and dove at him again.

"That crazy, idiot bird!" Kevin shouted, and in the next breath yelled, "Duck!"

The pigeon missed Kevin's head by inches. *Heh-heh-heh!* sounded a voice.

Kevin's mouth dropped open. "Ginnie! Did you hear that?" he cried, staring dumbfoundedly at the bird as it flew to a tree and landed on one of its top branches.

"Hear what?" Ginnie asked.

"He laughed!" Kevin said, pointing at the pigeon. "That pigeon actually laughed!"

3

EARLY THE NEXT MORNING Kevin and Ginnie were playing tennis on the town court. He was tired but had agreed to play with her after listening to her pleading that he practice for the better part of fifteen minutes.

The episode of the pigeon had been practically forgotten. No pigeon was known to laugh, Ginnie had told him. He just *thought* it had laughed.

After having that sensible sounding knowledge drummed into his head he really believed that it must have been something else he had heard the pigeon call. It couldn't have been laughter.

"You've got to develop your serve and your backhand," she now told him. "Those are your weak points. And don't you think for one minute that Roger Murphy doesn't know it!"

"What makes you think that I'll develop a champion serve and backhand by Friday?" he said, staring at her.

"Maybe not champion. But they'll be *better!*"

"O.K., O.K.," he said, yielding to her. What else could a guy do? Listen to her gripe at him all day? Anyway, even though she was younger than he, what she had observed about his serves and backhand strokes made sense.

She should know. She had started to play on a school team a whole year before he had even held a racket. It just wasn't in him to play any kind of sport while he was in the elementary grades. Conscious of his thin, reedlike body, he could never see himself as an athlete. Not until early last year, when Ginnie began to climb all over him about playing tennis, had he finally decided to take up the sport.

They rallied the ball back and forth across

the net. Finally Kevin said, "O.K. I'm warmed up."

He stopped the ball by bringing the racket up in a short sweeping arc and striking the ball near the top so that it dropped almost straight down in front of him. Then he caught it as it bounced up.

"Hey, that was neat, man!" Ginnie cried. "When did you develop *that?*"

Kevin shrugged. "I do it a lot while I practice knocking the ball against the house. It's no big deal."

"Well, *I* can't do it," she said.

Kevin stepped back behind the baseline, waited for Ginnie to get ready, then started to serve when Ginnie yelled, "Throw it up fairly high! Then bring your racket down on it as hard as you can!"

That's new? Kevin thought. *That's what I always try to do.*

He offered up the serve and drove the ball high over Ginnie's head. It landed way behind the line.

"You didn't come down with your racket!" Ginnie cried as she ran after it.

He tried again. This time the ball struck the top of the net, dropping on his side. "Two faults in a row," he said gloomily. "I'm doing just great, teacher."

"You're trying too hard," she told him.

His next serve was good. But out of the next five tries three were out of bounds. Disgusted with himself, he collapsed on the court, then rolled over on his back. He didn't even try to catch the ball that Ginnie returned to him.

"Something wrong, Kev?" Ginnie asked.

"Yeah," he said. "I'm sorry I ever let you talk me into playing this crazy game."

"Crazy game?" She came toward him, her eyes flashing fireworks. "Just because you haven't got the guts to learn the game well you call tennis a crazy game? Well, let me tell you something, Kevin Richard O'Toole. I think you're just *saying* that. You don't mean it, because you once told me that you love the game. But if that's the way you feel, that's the way you will feel about anything else you'll ever do with your life!"

With that she spun on her heels, her short blue skirt swirling about her slim body, and stamped off the court toward home. He followed her and when they got to their backyard, he heard her footsteps pounding up the porch steps, followed by a hard banging of the screen door.

He didn't blink an eye, but he stared up at the huge white clouds that drifted across the blue sky like a herd of giant elephants. What Ginnie had said hurt. But she was wrong, darn it. Dead wrong. He *would* amount to something when he grew up, no matter what career he chose.

A shadow flickered across his face. Then he saw a pigeon flying not too far above him. It swept around in a wide circle, then came gliding down toward him, wings spread out wide and its legs down like the landing gear of an airplane.

Kevin stared at it. It was the same pigeon

that had been at the tennis match! The same that had flown by him and Ginnie on their way home! What was the feathered little cuss up to, anyway?

The pigeon landed, closed its wings about its plump body and started to walk toward Kevin, its tail jerking back and forth with each step.

Kevin sat up, hardly believing what he saw. This bird really had nerve! *What is there about me that attracts me to him, anyway?* he thought. *Hey, bird, you're out of your cotton-pickin' mind. I'm no pigeon. Can't you tell?*

"Don't run, or scream, or do anything crazy. All right?"

Kevin's eyes almost popped out of his head. The words seemed to come out of the pigeon. But that was, of course, absurd. To find out who had spoken, he looked to one side, and then the other. *There was no one else around.*

He looked back at the pigeon.

"Keep your cool, Kevie," went on the pigeon. "And for Pete's sake don't faint. Promise?"

His heart beating like a drum, Kevin nodded. "I — I promise," he whispered.

The pigeon came to within an arm's length of Kevin and stopped. "I'm your great-great uncle, Rickard O'Toole," explained the pigeon seriously. "But call me Charlie. I hate that ridiculous name Rickard."

Kevin felt his skin crawl. "How — how can you be? You — you're a *pigeon*."

Charlie laughed. "I've been given another life. You know, reincarnated, boy. And I'm darn lucky. I might have come back into this world as a rat, you know. Or a skunk. A skunk! Ugh!" He chuckled then, his eyes brightening up with mischievous pleasure. "Now that would have been something, wouldn't it? I'd have a ball, especially with that Murphy family."

"Why that Murphy family?" asked Kevin, still not recovered from his first shock of meeting a talking pigeon.

"Why? You should ask," said Charlie. "I know this is news to you, but you are not the only one who doesn't like a Murphy."

"How do you know that?" said Kevin, staring at Charlie. "Anyway, it isn't that I don't *try* to like Roger. For some crazy reason he doesn't like *me*."

Charlie's eyes glinted. "You know why he doesn't? I'll tell you why. It's in the blood. It's like the old feud between the Hatfields and the McCoys. The Murphys and the O'Tooles hadn't got along with each other in a hundred and fifty years, ever since one of them Murphy guys stole a wagonload of wine from the O'Tooles."

"I never heard of that," said Kevin, surprised.

"Well, I've met quite a lot of old-timers since I've started this new life," said Charlie, "and that's what they tell me. Of course, some of them insist that it was the O'Tooles who stole the wagonload from the Murphys, but those who said that were Murphy confederates. Naturally they'd say that."

He paused, and Kevin let a grin spread over his face. *Naturally,* he thought, and almost said, *Charlie, you must have been a real card when you were Uncle Rickard O'Toole!*

25

"You're playing Roger on Friday, right?" said Charlie.

"Right," answered Kevin.

"Well, that's why I'm here," Charlie explained, settling comfortably on the ground with his legs under him. "Did your father ever tell you that I was almost a Wimbledon champion?"

"Why, yes. Yes, he did," Kevin said, suddenly remembering. There were a few other things that his father had told Kevin about his Great-Great Uncle Rickard too, but Kevin thought it was wise not to bring them up now.

"I was knocking down my opponents like a bowling ball knocks down tenpins," Charlie said. "Then I got it, but bad."

"Got what?" asked Kevin.

"Tennis elbow," said Charlie. "It finished me completely. And in those days there was nothing that would cure it. I was *finished*. I know I would have won at Wimbledon if that hadn't happened." He jerked his head to the left and riveted his right eye on Kevin so hard that

Kevin thought he was going to be hypnotized. "That's what you must watch out for, Kevie. Tennis elbow. It could ruin your playing tennis forever."

"But there is a cure for that now, isn't there, Uncle Rickard?" The instant he spoke he realized how ridiculous it sounded. Calling a pigeon Uncle Rickard. Anybody who might have heard him would think he had lost his marbles.

"*Charlie,*" said Charlie seriously. "Call me *Charlie. Never* Uncle Rickard. And never *Uncle* Charlie. Just *Charlie.* O.K.?"

"O.K. — Charlie."

"That's better." Charlie cleared his throat. "Sure there's a cure. But the old arm won't ever be the same again, and neither will you. You'll always worry about it, wondering if it will happen again. Keep it in mind, but now let's get down to business. Your sister, Ginnie, has been trying to teach you to play better tennis, and I commend her for that. She's a good, smart kid, Ginnie is. But she's got a lot to learn about the game, herself. Maybe, after I get through teaching you, you can give her a tip or two."

"Huh!" said Kevin. "That *would* be something."

"Of course it would. But don't be surprised. You *will* be teaching her if you'll listen to me. First off — "

Just then Kevin heard the squeak of the screen door hinges, and then the sound of Ginnie's footsteps coming down the porch steps.

"Oh-oh," said Charlie. "Here she comes. She was angry before so I'd better split. Don't say a word to her about me, O.K.? I don't want anybody to know about me except you. Promise?"

"I promise," said Kevin.

"Good." Charlie rose to his feet, spread his wings and took off, the tip of his left wing barely brushing against Kevin's face as he flew by.

4

Wasn't that our pigeon? I mean the one that's been pestering us?" said Ginnie, as she handed Kevin one of the two glasses of lemonade she had brought out.

"Yes, it was," said Kevin, and found it hard not to tell her who the pigeon really was. He still couldn't believe it. Reincarnation? He had thought that stuff — about somebody dying and returning to life in another form — was a lot of baloney. Charlie certainly proved that it wasn't.

"It seems to have taken to you," Ginnie observed. "I've never seen anything like it in my life."

"*That's* for sure," said Kevin, and took a couple of swallows of the lemonade.

"Want to play some more?" he asked as he emptied his glass and put it aside.

"I beg your pardon?" Ginnie's eyebrows shot up like a sprung shade. "Are you asking me if I want to play some more?"

"Foolish question, right?"

"You know it!" she cried. Quickly emptying her glass, she put it beside Kevin's, picked up her racket and the two tennis balls, then rested the head of the racket on the ground.

"Call it," she said.

"Rough side up," said Kevin.

She spun the racket. It slowed down, wobbled, and fell with the knotted strings side up.

They got on their bikes and rode quickly to the court. Luckily it was empty. "I'll take the north court," said Kevin. "The wind'll be at my back!"

They went to their respective places. Ginnie tossed up a ball and batted it across the net in a hard, solid drive. Kevin lobbed it back, placing it almost out of bounds to Ginnie's left side.

Sprinting after it, she slammed it back. Then they rallied the ball back and forth for almost half a minute before Ginnie gave the ball a smashing blow that drove it past Kevin for a point.

A voice yelled, "Nice shot, Gin! Maybe I should be playing you! I'd hate to skunk your brother!"

Kevin looked around at the speaker, Tommy Smith. With Tommy were Roger Murphy and Rusty Maxwell, the latter two grinning as if Tommy had said something funny.

"I'm scheduled to play Roger, not you," said Kevin.

"Well, ol' kid," Roger broke in, smiling crookedly, "the schedule has been changed. You're playing Tommy on Friday, and I'm playing Fats Monroe."

Kevin frowned. "Who said so?"

"Ben did. Fats is going on a vacation Saturday, the day he and I were scheduled to play."

"What happens if Tommy beats me?" Kevin asked.

"He plays Chuck Eagan on Wednesday. If

you win, you play Chuck. The winner of that match plays the winner of the Murphy-Monroe match next Saturday." Roger chuckled. "Fats hasn't beat me yet, Kev. Heck, if you lose to Tommy, and you really want to play me, just name the day and the hour. I'm ready, anytime."

Kevin felt it difficult to keep his cool. "I'll let you know," he said.

He looked across the court and saw Ginnie coming around the end of the net, wiping the sweat off her forehead. "I'm pooped," she said. "Let's quit."

He didn't think she was that tired. She was just saying that as an excuse to get rid of the guys.

Whether Tommy Smith read the implication in her statement or not, Kevin couldn't tell. But it sounded like it as the tall, blond boy ran a hand through his hair and grinned. "Come on, guys," he said. "We don't want to miss that movie."

The boys left, and Kevin looked at his sister.

"O.K. with you if we really quit? I just don't feel like playing anymore."

She shrugged. "I don't either," she admitted.

Ben Switzer called about half an hour later, informing Kevin of the schedule change. "So you'll be playing Tommy Smith on Friday, Kevin," he explained. "Be there promptly at one-thirty. O.K.?"

"O.K.," said Kevin.

It drizzled on Friday morning. By noon the clouds cleared away, the sun came out and the high humidity made the day hot and sticky. The small crowd that attended the match gave the boys a hand as Ben Switzer introduced them.

Kevin's mother and sister were sitting in the stands. He was disappointed that his father, an appliance repairman, had to work and couldn't be there. Both his mother and father played tennis, and sometimes joined in a doubles match with Kevin and Ginnie. He'd have to win today, and hope that his father could be there tomorrow.

Kevin won the spin and chose the north court instead of the chance to serve.

Tommy called, "Ready?"

"Ready!" replied Kevin.

Tommy tossed up a ball and belted it. *Thunk!* It curved out of bounds.

His next serve was just inside the sideline. Kevin slammed it back, driving it diagonally across the court to Tommy's right side. Tommy returned it straight across the net, forcing Kevin to bolt after it. He met the ball three-quarters of the way behind the net, swung and sliced it off to the left. He winced as he heard the crowd murmur. They were probably talking about how poorly he was playing.

"Fifteen–love!" sounded Ben Switzer's voice over a loudspeaker.

Tommy scored the next point too, belting a shot out of Kevin's reach. 30–love. He went on to win, twice earning points on Kevin's misplays.

He won the second game also.

What's the matter with me? Kevin asked

himself. *I just can't seem to get going. What will the crowd think?*

Just before Tommy began his first serve of the third game Kevin heard a soft flutter of wings. He looked up and saw Charlie diving low over the court, then zooming up and settling comfortably on a post, the same post he had perched on the other day.

Charlie winked at him and Kevin winked back. Maybe this was what he needed. Charlie.

Kevin scored on Tommy's first serve, got ahead of Tommy, and stayed ahead until the score was love–40. Then Tommy began to score and worked it up to a deuce game.

Kevin felt the life drizzle out of him. Sweat glistened on his face, but he was more anxious than tired.

"Buck up, boy," said Charlie. "You can't give up now."

The sound of Charlie's voice lifted Kevin's spirits a few notches. Tommy dealt a good serve, then rushed the net. Kevin hit the ball back, a soft shot that arced over the center of the net. Tommy returned it, and Kevin met it with a smashing blow that Tommy had no chance in the world to touch. Advantage Kevin.

"Attaboy," said Charlie.

Not so loud! Kevin wanted to yell at him.

Kevin took the next point to win the game. As he started off the court for the one-minute rest, Charlie glided down to him and stopped at his feet.

"Get down here," said Charlie. "Stroke my head as if I'm your pet or something."

Kevin did so, even though he felt foolish about it.

"Your problem is you, Kevie," said Charlie. "Instead of concentrating on the game, you're thinking about what the spectators are thinking of you. What they think if you make an error, and so on and so on. My boy, you've got to get your cotton-pickin' mind off that crowd and start concentrating on the game. You've got to watch that ball closely all the time and try to make your returns sure-fire. You can do that only by meeting the ball squarely and hitting it a little easier. Aim it where your opponent ain't. Get what I mean?"

"You're right about concentration, Charlie," admitted Kevin. "I just can't do it."

"You've *got* to do it, Kevie," Charlie said, jerking his head from one side to the other in order to look up at Kevin with both eyes. "That's number one in tennis. Without it you might as well forget it and take up tiddly-winks. And I'd hate to see you do that. I want you to play that Murphy kid and beat his britches off!"

"I'll do my best, Charlie."

"Hey, Kev!" yelled a voice Kevin recognized as Roger Murphy's. "What's with you and the pigeon?"

"Wouldn't *he* like to know," said Charlie. He winked at Kevin and took off, flying back up to his perch on the post.

KEVIN TRIED TO FOLLOW Charlie's advice as the fourth game of the first set got under way. He kept his eye on the ball as Tommy returned his serve, a sharp drive that headed straight for the baseline.

He waited, breathless. It struck just inside the line, and Kevin swung. Off balance, he met the ball with the throat of the racket, sending it dribbling toward the net. *Darn!* he thought angrily. A point for Tommy.

Kevin's next serve hit the net. He followed it up with a good one that Tommy returned without trouble. Then they stroked the ball back and forth, Kevin concentrating mainly on getting the ball back over the net as Charlie had advised, and not about what the fans might think of him if he made an error.

It wasn't easy, though. You can't change bad habits in one game, or in one set, or even in a dozen sets.

Then Tommy returned a ball that had bounced just inside his left sideline, and started to *walk* back toward the center of the court. Kevin, seeing his opportunity telegraphed to him, socked the ball hard to Tommy's opposite corner. Tommy sprinted after it but couldn't get within a mile of it. Kevin's point. 15–15.

Kevin also scored the next two points. Then Tommy scored by luck, the ball striking the top of the net and dropping over on Kevin's side. 40–30.

A minute later Kevin blasted the ball to Tommy's left side so that Tommy had to return with a backhand shot. The ball sliced out of bounds and Kevin won. The set was 2–all now.

Tommy started off cautiously in the fifth game, taking the first three points. Kevin wiped the sweat from his forehead as he shot a glance up at Charlie resting on top of the post. He saw Charlie jerk his head from side to side, then thought he heard Charlie say, "Be the aggressor, boy. Wear him down."

Sounds O.K., Charlie. But what if I wear down first?

He returned Tommy's serve beautifully. Tommy returned his just as beautifully. Then Kevin belted the ball a solid blow, bringing up his racket as he struck to give the sphere a topspin.

The stroke worked. The ball shot over the net and bounced so sharply past Tommy that he wasn't able to touch it. Four more points on hard drives gave Kevin the game and put him in the lead, 3 games to 2.

It was his turn to serve now, and he got a fault on his first try. The next was almost outside, hitting the sideline for a score that was pure luck. Tommy swung too late at it, apparently thinking that it might hit outside the line. 15–love.

"Pretty lucky, O'Toole," Roger Murphy said, just loud enough for Kevin to hear.

Kevin failed again to get his first serve right. His second was better. Tommy returned it, and for half a dozen strokes the boys played errorless ball.

Then Kevin saw his chance to be *aggressive* again, and blasted the ball to the corner behind Tommy. 30–love.

Whether it was the shot or the score, Tommy's balloon was pricked. Kevin took the next two points, winning his first love game of the match. Tommy couldn't seem to get out of his slump and lost the set, 6–2.

As the boys walked to the bench to rest, Kevin looked up at Charlie and saw the pigeon's right eye close and open in a pleased wink.

"Good match, Kevie," said Charlie. "You follow instructions like a real pro."

Kevin smiled. "I guess I owe you . . ." he

started to say, then paused. If the fans heard him talking to a pigeon they'd think that he was ready for the funny farm!

Even though the rest was only for a minute, Kevin was grateful for it. He really needed it. The heat was torture.

"Kevin!"

He turned and saw Ginnie leaning forward in her seat, her hands cupped around her mouth. "Finish him off in the next set!"

"Ginnie!" said her mother, grabbing Ginnie's arm and pulling her back. "Don't be so cruel!"

"What's cruel about that?" said Ginnie.

Kevin looked away, grinning. He knew that Mom had to undergo a lot of embarrassment quite often because of her daughter's courage to say whatever was on her mind.

As the boys changed sides for the start of the second set, Kevin saw that Charlie wasn't on the post. He glanced around to see if Charlie had discovered another perch. He had not.

Then Kevin glimpsed a pigeon flying high in the distance, and figured that Charlie was just exercising his wings. After all, sitting on a small flat spot for a couple of hours would tire any old body. Nonetheless Kevin hoped the remarkable bird would return soon.

Tommy, serving first, failed to get the initial shot over the net. His second was good. He seemed to have regained a lot of his composure, and started to score points on hard-hit shots that Kevin got a racket on but hit out of bounds. Tommy took the first three games, out-playing, out-hitting, out-shining Kevin as if he had been saving up all his tricks and skill for this second set.

But something happened to his playing in the fourth game. Kevin guessed it was fatigue. Tommy had been doing a lot of running in the first three games and in the heat might have run himself ragged. Anyway, Kevin once again became the aggressor and the tide turned. He took the next four games in a row.

Then fatigue weakened him too. *Ease up, Kev,* warned his conscience. *Maybe this is exactly what Tommy wants you to do — get all bushed so he can take you to the cleaners in the next three games.*

Kevin listened to his conscience and took it easy. Tommy took the game. 4–all.

Ginnie clattered down the stands and sat next to Kevin during the one-minute rest period. "You're playing a good game, Kev!"

"You're just trying to make me feel good. But thanks, anyway," he said.

Both boys went into the next game strong. But it was Tommy who won it on a lob over Kevin's head. 5–4, Tommy.

Just before Kevin began to serve the next game he heard a whisper of wings near him and the next thing he knew Charlie was perched on his right shoulder.

"Charlie!" Kevin cried sharply. "Where have you been?"

"You need some sound advice, boy, so I came back," said Charlie into his ear. "You can take that Smith kid if you'll listen to old Charlie. Will you listen?"

"I'm listening, I'm listening!" answered

45

Kevin anxiously. "But hurry, will you? The crowd will wonder what in heck's going on!"

The crowd was already wondering what in heck was going on. A buzzing had started up among them, mixed with a ripple of laughter.

"You've got to be more aggressive," advised Charlie in that funny, cooing pigeon voice of his. "Hit the ball behind him. He's a poor backhand shot, and that's what you have to work on. O.K.?"

"O.K. Now get, will you, Charlie, before I'm disqualified for holding up the game?"

"Attaboy," said Charlie, starting to lift his wings to take off. "Spunk! That's what I like. See you, boy."

Charlie flew off, leaving a very embarrassed Kevin looking after him. Instantly a thunder of applause rose from the fans, mixed with a chorus of yells.

"Who's your friend, Kevin?"

"Why didn't you give *him* the racket?"

Then, the inevitable clincher, "Is he your coach, Kevin? Ha! Ha!"

Man, if I told you he was, you'd die!

Kevin followed Charlie's advice as well as he could, trying to hit the ball behind Tommy whenever the opportunity arose. But his anxiety doomed him. Most of the shots landed either against the net or out of bounds.

Tommy won the game, and the set.

6

AFTER THE TEN-MINUTE rest period both boys appeared fresh and full of pep. Kevin wished it was all over with, though. Fresh-looking he might be, but his arms and legs felt as if spikes were driven into them.

He lost the first game by an embarrassingly wide margin; he didn't score a point.

The next game was better, but Tommy won it. Game–30.

"I think you're *too* aggressive," said Ginnie during the one-minute rest period. "You're playing into his hands."

There you go, thought Kevin in utter confusion. *Charlie tells me to be more aggressive and she tells me I'm too aggressive. Maybe I'd be smarter to ignore their advice and play my own way.*

Tommy served the third game. Kevin took Ginnie's advice and relaxed a bit. Twice the game went into the advantage stage for him, and both times Tommy tied it up. Then Kevin took two points in a row and won it. 2–1, Tommy.

Kevin won the next game too, not only tying up the score, but proving something he had been told in the process. *Don't be too aggressive. Just hit the ball over the net. Let your opponent drive it back as hard as he wants to. Count on him to make the errors.*

He took the game, and finally the set, 6–2.

He ran over and shook hands with Tommy. Then, as he started off the court amid loud applause from the fans, he heard a sudden flutter of wings and there was Charlie, settling on his shoulder.

"Nice game, Kevie!" said Charlie, tickling

Kevin's right ear with the tip of his wing. "You played that last set like your great old uncle used to! You were marvelous, boy! Just marvelous!"

"Thanks, Charlie," Kevin said, and thought: *Like my great old uncle used to? You sure about that, Charlie? I thought you were the aggressive type!*

"See you later, Kevie," Charlie said. "Right now you're in for some congratulations from your happy fans." With that he flew off, and Kevin felt the dig of his sharp claws on his shoulder.

"See you, Charlie," said Kevin. Then he turned to meet his sister, mother and a host of other people who came to offer him their congratulations.

They made quite a fuss over him. He liked it, yet, *Wonder what they would've done if I had lost?* he thought.

That evening Charlie flew in while Kevin was lying on the smooth, close-cut, cool lawn.

The sun was just beginning to set, a big red disk with a veil of cloud streamers lying across the face of it.

"Tch! Tch!" muttered Charlie. "What a life!"

Kevin grinned. "Don't tell *me* what a life. I think *you've* got the life. Wish I could fly, go anywhere anytime I please, and not think about what clothes to wear. Man, I'd have a ball."

Charlie chuckled. "That's being envious, boy. And envy is the root of a lot of heart-aches."

"Now you sound like my third grade teacher," said Kevin. "Shall I bring out a black-board?"

"Tch! Tch!" said Charlie again. "I'm just tell-ing you these things for your own good, Kevie. Having lived a good many years as a human, I learned what kind of flowers were safe to pluck and what kind weren't. Envy is far from being a rose."

"I'm sorry, Charlie," said Kevin. "I didn't mean to be smart."

"Forget it. The fact is, you're right. I'm

happy in this new life of mine. It does have a lot of advantages over being a human. But the trouble is, I still love tennis. That's the advantage you have over me. Who'd think of making a tennis racket for a pigeon? Anyway, if anybody was crazy enough to try it, how could I ever hold onto the darn thing?"

Kevin laughed. "I guess you're right, Charlie. There are advantages in being a human being *and* being a pigeon." He rolled over and looked Charlie in the left eye. "Can I ask you a very personal question?"

"Shoot," said Charlie.

"Do you have any pigeon friends? You're not the *only* pigeon who used to be a human being, are you?"

Charlie let out a peal of laughter. "Of course not, boy! I have several friends!"

"Where are they? I've only seen you around here."

Charlie ruffled his feathers in what Kevin presumed to be a shrug. "That's because they preferred to stay back there in the city, under that big church steeple near the courtyard. I was never much of a city kid. Not too many tennis courts there. But, frankly, living under that church steeple has something appealing about it. We could find food easy enough. You'd be surprised how anxious people are to feed us. It's toughest in winter, of course. But we manage to get all we need."

"Do you play games? What kind of fun do you have?"

Kevin listened eagerly, realizing that he must be one of the very, *very* few lucky people in the whole wide world who could be having a heart-to-heart talk with a pigeon. At least, he had never heard of anyone ever talking to a pigeon before.

"Sure we play games," replied Charlie seriously. "Follow the Leader is one of our favorites. We have some good fliers, you know. As a matter of fact, some of those guys used to fly the old Spads and Handley Pages during World War One. You ought to hear the stories they tell."

"Spads and Handley Pages?" Kevin frowned. "Are they airplanes?"

"Are they airplanes?" Charlie almost died laughing. "They *were* airplanes, boy! Spads were American fighters and Handley Pages were heavy bombers. Oh, they were airplanes, all right! And the guys who flew them were real fliers!"

A voice, coming from the house, interrupted them. "Kevin! Who are you talking to?"

Before Kevin could turn around he heard Ginnie's feet rattling down the steps.

"Oh-oh," said Charlie. "It's that kid sister of yours."

Kevin rolled over onto his back and looked up at Ginnie as she stopped beside him, hands on her hips. She looked from him to Charlie, an expression on her face Kevin could describe only as sheer wonderment.

"You — you weren't carrying on a conversation with that pigeon, were you?" she said. "You — you haven't gone out of your mind?"

Kevin tightened his lips and looked at Char-

lie. *Well, Charlie, old uncle, what shall I tell her? She heard us talking. If I deny it, she'll really think I'm crazy. Maybe she'll tell Mom and Dad and the next thing you know I'll be in a hospital having my head examined.*

Charlie met Kevin's intense gaze, then hopped over close to Kevin and whispered into his ear, "Tell her the whole story, and make her promise not to tell another living soul. That's going to be tough for her to do, but we have to count on it. O.K.?"

"O.K.," said Kevin. Looking up at Ginnie, he saw her eyebrows jerked upward in surprise and her face turning the color of paper.

Kevin said gently, "Sit down, Gin. I've got something to tell you, and you've got to keep it to yourself. Forever. Think you can do that?"

She stared at him. Then her head bobbed as she sat down, curling her legs under her. "I — I think so," she whispered.

"You — you know what reincarnation is, don't you?" Kevin asked her.

"Reincarnation?" She frowned. "I've heard of it."

"O.K. It's when a person dies and his soul enters another body," Kevin explained. "The body could be that of an insect, or an animal, or even a bird. Different religious sects believe in it."

Ginnie's eyes seemed to grow even wider as they hopped from Kevin to Charlie and back to Kevin. She straightened her back as if something was crawling down it.

A chuckle broke the tense silence, and both Kevin and Ginnie looked at Charlie. The expression on Ginnie's face was one of utmost surprise.

"What he's driving at, my dear Ginnie," Charlie chimed in as a loving old uncle might, "is that I used to be your Great-Great Uncle Rickard O'Toole. And after my death I returned in the form you see before you. Not as handsome, perhaps, but what can you expect of a pigeon?"

Ginnie's face paled. Then slowly her color came back, and a happy smile came over her face.

"I can't believe it!" she cried softly. "Oh, I just can't believe it!"

"You might as well believe it," said Charlie. "Because it's true. But don't shout the news so loud that the whole world will hear you. This has got to be a secret just between us three. Remember that."

Ginnie shook her head vigorously, no longer straight-backed nor as scared-looking as she was when she had first heard him talk. "I'll remember that, Uncle . . ."

"Charlie," interrupted Charlie quickly. "Never call me uncle anything. It's just Charlie. All my pigeon friends call me Charlie, and that's what I want you and Kevin to call me, too. O.K.?"

"O.K.," said Ginnie, bobbing her head so that her hair fell over her face and she had to whip it back. "Oh, Charlie! I'm so happy to meet you!"

"O.K., O.K. But just keep your voice down, for Pete's sake," reminded Charlie, sounding a bit cranky. "Now let's talk about tennis for a while. That's the real reason I'm here." He cocked his head to the right so that his left eye focused on Kevin. "You're playing Roger Murphy next Saturday, right?"

"Not unless I beat Chuck Eagan on Wednesday," said Kevin.

Charlie chuckled. "Oh, you'll beat him. It's that Roger kid you'll have trouble with. I've watched him. He plays like his great uncle used to."

"Which great uncle?" Ginnie broke in.

"Sanford," said Charlie. "Sanford Wallington Murphy. What do you think of *that* handle? Anyway, Wally — as we used to call him — had two main weaknesses which only a few of us were able to detect. A low drive that landed near his feet, and a drive hit to his forehand side. He had trouble returning either one."

"His *forehand* side?" Kevin frowned. "Are you sure about that, Charlie?"

"As sure as I'm standing here," replied Charlie. "You see, Rog has probably done the same thing old Wally did. He's worked on his backhand stroke so much that he paid too little attention to his forehand."

Kevin shrugged. "Makes sense — I guess," he said.

"Of course it makes sense," said Charlie. "Remember those two . . ."

"Hey!" a loud voice interrupted. "Isn't that the same pigeon that was at the tennis match this afternoon?"

"Oh-oh," muttered Charlie. "It's the enemy. Roger, himself. See you kids later. I'm getting famished, anyway."

He sprang up, spread out his gray-white wings, and flew off. Kevin watched him as he climbed higher and higher, gradually diminishing into a dot and then vanishing into the fast growing dusk.

7

Roger came into the yard, blowing a piece of bubble gum to the size of a baseball. *Explode, gum!* Kevin thought. *Stick to his face! Better yet, stick to his mouth so that he can't open it!*

The gum exploded with a loud burst. But that was as far as the sticky substance went in satisfying Kevin's wish. *Rotten luck. Bet if it was me the darn stuff would stick to my face.*

"As I was saying," said Roger. "Isn't that the same . . ."

"It is," Ginnie cut him off short. "And I guess you know now what pigeons think of you."

Roger grinned that crooked grin of his, and Kevin wondered if a clean sock on the side of his jaw might straighten it out.

"Well, I'm not one for pigeons," Roger remarked. "Not for any kind of birds, for that matter."

He stuck his hands into his rear pants pockets and started to rock back and forth on his heels.

"He seems to be pretty friendly with you two," he observed. "What have you got that nobody else has, anyway?"

"A friendly face," Ginnie answered.

"We talk his language," Kevin said.

"What? Coo coo?" said Roger, and doubled over, laughing.

I walked into that one, Kevin thought as he saw the disgusted look that Ginnie gave him. Finally Roger straightened up. "I suppose you've got a name for him."

"Of course," said Kevin.

"No kidding. What is it?"

"None of your bus . . ." Ginnie started to say,

but Kevin interrupted, "No, we'll tell him, Gin," he said. "We won't have to worry about losing Charlie as a friend just because we tell Roger *that* much about him."

Roger frowned. "Charlie? Is that what you call him? And what do you mean about telling me *that* much about him?"

Now, Kevin thought, *it's my turn to laugh.* And he did.

"Just sleep on that for a while, Roger," he said. "So long. I've got some chores to do."

"Better practice up for that game with Chuck," Roger reminded him. "Otherwise we might not be playing each other this year."

Kevin's ears turned red. What Roger meant, of course, was that Kevin might not beat Chuck Eagan in their forthcoming match and earn a match with Roger.

Losing to Chuck didn't necessarily mean that an O'Toole-Murphy match could not be played. It could, if only to satisfy their egos. Especially Roger's. But it was Kevin's hope to play the cocky Roger properly.

"Don't worry," said Kevin. "You and I will play, all right. You can bet your big fat bubble gum on that."

He turned and walked up to the house, expecting to hear that familiar Roger Murphy laugh. But he didn't. All he heard was the door closing quietly behind him as Ginnie followed him into the house, then Ginnie's surprising comment, "I feel sorry for him. Can you believe it?"

He looked at her. Sure enough she was either putting on a command performance, or the expression on her pixy face was real.

"No," he said. "But then again, knowing you, I guess I can."

Two days slipped by. Charlie had not been seen since Roger had broken up his conversation with Kevin and Ginnie and he had flown off into the wild blue yonder. Where was he? Why hadn't he come around in the last two days?

Kevin got worried.

"I can't figure it out, Gin," he said on the third day of Charlie's absence. "He's never been away from us this long before."

"Maybe he's gone back to his friends at that old church steeple," she said.

"Maybe. Shall we go find out?"

"It's the only way," she said.

They got permission from their mother to take a bus to downtown New Laswell. It was only a two-block walk from where they got off the bus to the church where Charlie had said he and his friends congregated. Good thing that Charlie had described the church as being near a courtyard, otherwise it might have been days before they would have found the right one.

"That's it," Ginnie said, pointing at the church steeple sticking up into the sky like a long spike. "Look at the pigeons. There must be hundreds."

"Look at those diving down like bombers," said Kevin. "They must be the ones who used to fly the Spads and Handley Pages."

They approached the courtyard.

"How can we tell which is Charlie?" said Ginnie wonderingly. "They all look alike."

"Don't worry," Kevin assured her. "If he's there he'll see us and come."

They stood watching the pigeons assembled on the roof, under the cornices, and flying around the steeple and the courtyard. There were benches in the courtyard with people sitting on them, some holding bags of peanuts which they fed to the pigeons that fluttered fearlessly around them.

"I see what Charlie means about being well fed," Kevin observed. "Guess it's not a bad life, at that."

"For a pigeon," Ginnie said.

They hung around for ten minutes, according to an electric clock on a corner of the New Laswell National Bank.

"He isn't here," Kevin said, a lump coming to his throat. "We might as well go home."

They took a bus, neither saying more than a few words during the whole ride.

"What are we going to do?" asked Ginnie.

"I don't know," answered Kevin.

It wasn't until they were off the bus that Ginnie seemed to find her tongue again. "Let's ask Mom," she said. "Maybe she can think of something."

Mrs. O'Toole was stirring up a cake batter when the kids got home.

"Well," she said, surprised. "You two sure made it back in a hurry. Did you find Charlie?"

"No," said Kevin, getting a whiff of the sweet, mouth-watering smell. "That's what we want to see you about, Mom. We're stuck. We don't know what else to do."

"Have you checked with some of the people in the neighborhood?" she asked, looking at her two offspring with her wide blue eyes.

Kevin shrugged. "No. But what could they tell us? Pigeons all look alike to them."

"Maybe something happened to your pigeon and somebody might have heard about it," she said. "I hope for your sake and Charlie's that nothing has happened to him, of course. But

I've seen kids with B-B guns. And a pigeon makes a pretty good-size target."

The thought sent chills scurrying like mice up and down Kevin's back. "That's right, Ma," he said. "And Charlie, being a gutsy pigeon, would let himself be an easy target for any dumb kid with a gun."

He headed for the door. "Come on, Gin. Let's get moving. Thanks, Ma! We *knew* you'd come up with something!"

T<small>HEY WALKED FOUR BLOCKS</small> down Colvin
Street, asking every kid they met — whether
they knew him or not — if he had seen or heard
of an injured pigeon. Usually they'd get the
same look, and the same answer, "No."

They turned left on Mitchell and continued
the procedure, sometimes going a full block
without spotting a single kid.

"Can't be they're *all* watching that stupid
boob tube," Ginnie said.

"Never know," Kevin replied.

They had turned left on Carpenter Street
when a thought struck Kevin that made him

realize how stupid *they* were for confining their questions only to kids.

"Hey, what's the matter with us?" he said, grabbing Ginnie's elbow and stopping in the middle of the sidewalk. "What's wrong with our asking grownups, too?"

Ginnie grinned sheepishly. "Why didn't *I* think of that?" she said.

"Sure," said Kevin. "Come on. From now on we'll ask every living soul we meet if they've seen or heard about Charlie."

The first two people they met were grownups. Neither was of any help. The next person they met was another kid, a dark-haired boy carrying a baseball glove and a ball.

Kevin, almost certain what the kid's answer would be, popped the question anyway. "We've lost our pet pigeon," he said for the umpteenth time. "Have you seen or heard anything about one around here?"

The kid's eyes opened a fraction wider. "Yeah," he said. "Somebody shot one a couple of days ago."

Kevin's heart stopped. Then it started up again, pumping harder than ever. "Wh-where is it? Who shot it? Did he use a B-B gun?"

"*Is it dead?*" Ginnie asked in a husky whisper.

The kid looked at both of them again before answering. "I don't think so. I'm not sure."

"Where is it?" Kevin said. "Do you know who's got it?"

"Yeah." The kid pointed at a green, white-shuttered house a short distance down the street. "It's at that house there. Eagan's."

"Eagan's?" Kevin's heart received another jolt. "You mean Chuck Eagan's?"

"Yeah. You know him?"

"Know him? I sure do! I'm playing tennis with him on Wednesday!"

"*He* shot the pigeon?" Ginnie said, her voice ready to break. "Chuck did?"

The kid's head bobbed up and down as if it were on a spring.

"Come on, Gin!" cried Kevin, already heading for Chuck's house. "Thanks, kid!"

He was at the front door before Ginnie was

even starting up the porch steps. He knocked on it, trying to keep from falling apart as he certainly might have were he not well secured at the joints.

The door opened. A tall, red-haired woman stood there; her steel-blue eyes coldly looked them over.

"Sorry," she said. "Whatever you're selling I have plenty to last me for weeks. Good . . ."

"We're not salesmen, Mrs. Eagan," Kevin interrupted before she was able to close the door. "We're the O'Tooles. I'm Kevin and this is my sister, Ginnie."

The stern eyes softened as if he had spoken the magic word. "Oh, yes," said Mrs. Eagan, placing a finger against the cleft in her chin. "You're to play tennis with Charles."

"That's right. Is he in?"

"Yes. Just a minute."

She left. A minute later a tall, skinny kid in a T-shirt with the names of universities printed in all directions on it came to the door. "Hi," he said.

"Hi, Chuck," said Kevin. "It's about that pigeon you shot. Did you kill it? Do you still have it?"

"Why?"

"We — we'd just like to look at it," said Ginnie.

"It's O.K., if that's what you want to know."

"Can we look at it? Please?" said Kevin.

Chuck thought a minute. "O.K.," he said finally, and went back into the house. A moment later he was back, carrying —

"Charlie!" Kevin cried, a lump suddenly clogging his throat. "It *is* you!"

He reached for Charlie, who glanced up at him and then at Ginnie with a surprised look. His wings fluttered as he started to rise, then went limp as he settled back in Chuck's arms, his beak open, his tongue trembling.

"Is this the pigeon that's been coming to the tennis matches?" Chuck asked.

"Yes," said Kevin. "He's our pet. We've been looking all over for him."

"You — you didn't know he was our pet?" inquired Ginnie, a tone of suspicion in her voice.

74

"No. Why should I? All pigeons look alike."

Ginnie shrugged. "Well, I just thought . . ." Her voice trailed off.

"Yeah, I know," said Chuck. "You thought that I might have shot your pet pigeon to hurt Kevin so that he'd be no good in the game we're playing on Wednesday. Ain't that right?"

Kevin stared at him. "Now wait a minute, Chuck."

"Well, that's what she meant, isn't it?" Chuck snapped.

"Yes, that's what I meant, Chuck," Ginnie admitted, "and I don't want to accuse you of anything, but it's dumb to shoot *any* bird."

"You know how Ginnie is, Chuck," said Kevin. "Right or wrong she always speaks her mind."

Ginnie shot her brother a cold stare, then smiled at Chuck. "Thank goodness he wasn't killed," she said, and reached for Charlie.

Chuck pulled him back. "His right wing is busted," he said. "I've put a splint on it."

"You — you *are* going to give him back to us, aren't you?" Kevin said, fear gripping him at the dreadful thought that Chuck just might not want to. "After all, he is ours."

"We'll forget that you shot him," Ginnie said. "We won't tell anybody."

"I don't care about that," Chuck said. "A lot of guys know it already."

He glanced past Kevin. A second later footsteps sounded behind Kevin and a voice said, "Is that Charlie, your pet pigeon?"

Both Ginnie and Kevin turned around at the same time. Neither one was overly pleased at the sight of the newcomer who, by now, was on the porch, his hands pressed into his rear pants pockets.

"That's right," said Kevin.

"I told Chuck that he looked like your pet pigeon," said Roger Murphy. "But they all look alike. You sure it's yours?"

"No doubt about it," said Kevin. "Look what he does when I reach for him."

As Kevin reached for Charlie, Charlie leaned toward him, as if eager to go to him. "See that?" said Kevin. "Now you try it."

Roger did. Charlie backed away, turning his

head and cooing indignantly. Laughter broke from Ginnie, Kevin and Chuck.

"Guess that proves it, all right," said Chuck. "O.K., Kev. Here, take him."

Happily, Kevin took Charlie into his arms. Boy, how he ached to squeeze the adorable bird to him to show him how thrilled he was that he had him back.

"See you Wednesday," said Chuck, as Kevin and Ginnie started off the porch.

"Right," said Kevin. In a softer tone he said, "Got to get you home so I can take a look at your wounded wing, Charlie."

THE CRUD GOT ME WITH one rifle shot while I was perched on a tree in his backyard," Charlie said angrily. "It feels as bad as the tennis elbow did when I was a human."

"What in heck were you doing on a tree in his backyard?" asked Kevin, looking at the splint clamped to Charlie's right wing. It looked like a good first aid job. Better than he could have done himself.

"Spying," confessed Charlie. "I was checking him out."

"Checking him out?" Kevin echoed. "You mean you were watching him practice tennis in his backyard?"

"You get the picture," said Charlie, his head bobbing. "Well, you want to beat him, don't you? You want to play that Murphy kid, don't you? And beat him?"

Kevin shook his head. "Charlie, you're impossible. Just plain impossible. You're lucky you weren't killed, you stupid pige . . . Oh-oh. I'm sorry, Charlie. I didn't mean that."

"Yes, you did, and you're right," said Charlie. "But I was looking out for you. I really want you to beat those kids, Kevie. Nothing will ever please me more during the rest of my pigeon life than your playing Roger Murphy and beating him."

"You must have really disliked that ancestor of his, didn't you?" said Kevin, trying hard to control a chuckle.

"Can you blame me?" Charlie said hotly. "He was a stinkpot, I tell you. A stinkpot through and through."

Kevin smiled and stroked Charlie's soft, velvet-like feathers. "I'll do my best, Charlie," he promised. "But what if I beat Chuck and

Roger beats me? He's pretty good, you know."

"Then I would wish you a tennis elbow. No, no! I take that back!" Charlie said quickly. "I'm sorry. I can't wish tennis elbow on my worst enemy. Except Wally Murphy. And it's too late for that. Just beat him, will you, Kevie? Let's forget the consequences till later. O.K.?"

Kevin grinned. "O.K. I think that's the best idea, Charlie. By the way, *did* you find out what Chuck's weaknesses are?"

"A little. He was playing in his driveway with Roger, as you know," Charlie said. "But they weren't playing seriously. I couldn't learn much other than he seemed rather weak with his serves. They were only fooling around, and the next thing I knew he had gone into the house and come out with his rifle. It's a good thing I started off just as he took aim and fired, otherwise I might've been a dead pigeon."

Game time between Kevin and Chuck Eagan was at five o'clock on Wednesday. Chuck won the choice to serve or the side of the court. He chose to serve. Kevin chose the north side, noting that a soft breeze was blowing from that direction.

Chuck's first serve hit the net for a fault. He tried again, this time driving the ball over the net directly at Kevin. Kevin returned it with a light stroke, biding his time to get better warmed up. He had promised himself that he would do his best to beat Chuck, and felt that he had a good chance to do it. At least a better chance than he would have against Roger.

But beating Roger would earn the feather in his cap. Charlie would be thrilled to pieces then.

Don't push your luck, O'Toole. Let's take them one at a time, O.K.?

A poor backhand return on Chuck's part earned Kevin his first point. He scored another on a double fault, a break for him. Love–30. Then Chuck evened it up with a solid drive that just hit the left sideline. And another that was so easy to hit that Kevin, in his eagerness to get it just over the net, drove it *into* the net instead.

Kevin won the next two points on faults, and took the game.

He served the second game and lost it game–15, mostly because of his poor serves. It was 1–all now.

He scored better in the third game, but not much. Someone seemed to have moved the net up a few inches. He just couldn't get the ball over it. Chuck 2; Kevin 1.

It was Kevin's serve now. His first try was a let. His next was better than he expected, for it bounced sideways, fooling Chuck completely. Kevin's fans cheered him on the play, though he knew that the bounce was a fluke.

Luck seemed to return to Chuck during the rest of the game. He took it with Kevin not scoring a point. Chuck 3; Kevin 1.

You're choking up, O'Toole. You're supposed to take this match. Remember? You promised yourself and Charlie that you would. Let's get on the ball, shall we?

Chuck took the next one, too.

Kevin, determined to make a better show-ing, bounced back with two wins in a row. Chuck 4; Kevin 3.

And then it happened. Chuck went after a hard smashing drive to his left side, swinging at the ball with a backhand stroke. He never touched the ball. His swing was half-way through when he stumbled, fell and stayed down on the court, writhing with pain.

10

THE ANKLE SEEMED to be sprained. Ben Switzer made the judgment after feeling it and finding it slightly swollen. It was really sore, too, according to the way Chuck twinged when Ben squeezed it.

"I'll take you home," Ben said. "A cold compress right away will help it a lot."

"My parents are here," said Chuck, a pained look on his face. "They'll take me home."

Kevin saw a tall, heavy-built man stepping down through the widely scattered fans, the boards bending under his weight. He approached Chuck who was standing up now, favoring his injured ankle.

"Tough luck, son," the man said, picking Chuck up in his arms like a toothpick. "What happens now, Ben? Does he lose the game?"

"We have a rule in our by-laws," said Ben. "If the match isn't continued within four days after an accident or an injury, it goes to the opponent."

"You mean that if Chuck's ankle doesn't heal up in that time the O'Toole boy wins the game?"

"That's right," Ben said.

Kevin, overhearing Ben's answer, knew right away what a certain kid would think if Chuck's ankle didn't heal up within four days. *What an easy way to win a match, O'Toole. But you'd like to win 'em all that way, wouldn't you?*

"Mr. Switzer," said Kevin, "can I say something?"

"You sure can, Kev."

"I'd rather wait for Chuck's ankle to heal than to win the match by a forfeit," he said, looking directly into Ben Switzer's eyes. "I don't care if it takes a week, or two weeks."

Ben's eyes lit up and a smile spread across his face. "Well, that's mighty big of you, Kevin. But the rule says — "

"Then I won't play Roger Murphy," Kevin broke in. "I won't play him unless I beat Chuck — if he doesn't beat me, that is," he added softly.

The men looked at each other. "Well, I guess that decides it," Ben said. "But let's hope that it won't take more than a few days for Chuck's ankle to heal. Suppose that I leave it up to you, Ed, to call me when you think Chuck's ready to play again?"

Mr. Eagan's face cracked into a broad smile. "I'll do that. And thanks, Kevin. You're a real square-shooting boy."

Ben announced to the fans that the match had to be discontinued because of an injury to Chuck's ankle, but that it would continue after the ankle had healed. They applauded briefly, then started to leave the stands, an air of disappointment hanging around them.

"Isn't there a four-day ruling governing injuries?" asked Kevin's father as they walked home together — he, his wife, Kevin and Ginnie.

"Yes, there is," answered Kevin. "But I told Mr. Switzer that I wouldn't take the game on a forfeit."

"Why not? You'd be breaking the rule if you didn't, wouldn't you?"

"Well — I told him that I wouldn't play Roger Murphy unless I played the match out with Chuck."

Gee, Dad, did you have to squeeze it out of me? You make me feel like a Boy Scout shooting for a merit badge.

"Oh, so that's it," said Mr. O'Toole. "Hmmm."

A call from Ben the next day revealed some good news. Chuck's ankle had not been sprained. It had just twisted enough to make it painful. "Chuck will be ready to play in a couple of days, Kevin," Ben said.

"Gee, that's great, Mr. Switzer," said Kevin. "Then we can play out the match on Saturday?"

"That's right. Saturday. Four o'clock O.K.?"

"Four o'clock will be fine, Mr. Switzer. When will the winner play the winner of the Murphy-Monroe match?"

"A week from Saturday. Also at four o'clock."

"Thanks, Mr. Switzer," said Kevin. "Mom!" he yelled, after hanging up. "That was Mr. Switzer! Chuck's ankle wasn't sprained after all! It was just twisted! We're going to play off the match on Saturday at four o'clock!"

"Good," said Mrs. O'Toole, coming into the kitchen from the dining room. "And I'm not deaf. At least, not yet."

"Sorry, Mom."

"Maybe Dad will get there in time after work to see at least one set. He thinks you're pretty good, you know."

"He does?"

"Uh-huh." She smiled and wrapped an arm around his shoulders. "He hasn't been able to see you play much, and was surprised how well you handled yourself in those games against Chuck."

"I wish Chuck hadn't hurt his ankle," he said

dismally. "If I beat him now, everybody will say he was handicapped."

"But he won't be," said his mother. "He'll be as good as if nothing had happened to him."

"I know. But everybody won't see it that way, Mom."

She squeezed his shoulder and kissed him on the forehead. "Don't worry about it. And don't think about it when you're on the court with Chuck. Play to win, and you will."

He grinned weakly. *You're something, Ma, you know that? You're really something.*

He went out on the porch where he kept Charlie safe and warm in a box, and found him asleep.

"Hey," he said, giving the top of the box a rapid tattoo. "Are you going to sleep all day?"

Charlie jerked awake, shook his head and focused a sleepy eye on Kevin. "Dummy," he said. "You ruined a beautiful dream."

Kevin laughed. "Sorry about that. What were you dreaming?"

"That's my business."

"Boy, you're sure friendly this morning. What can I get you?"

"Steak," said Charlie. "With all the trimmings."

"Rare, medium, or well done?"

Charlie cocked his head around and focused his other eye on Kevin. He chuckled.

"You know, Kevie, if I didn't know you better I'd think you were really serious."

Kevin laughed again and ran a hand over Charlie's velvet-soft head.

"Corn coming up, Charlie," he said, and walked away to get Charlie's lunch.

11

THE TENNIS MATCH CONTINUED where it had left off, with Chuck Eagan leading Kevin four games to three.

The eighth game started with Kevin serving. His first try was good, and so was Chuck's return. As the ball shot back and forth over the net, Kevin took notice of Chuck's moves. Nothing in the way Chuck got around and batted the ball indicated that he had injured his ankle at all.

But I can't ignore the fact that he has injured it, Kevin told himself. *Chuck can be a hard-headed kid at times. Maybe he still feels a little pain but won't admit it.*

Nonetheless Chuck won the game, game–30. It was 5–3 now, in his favor.

Kevin came back hard and took the next two games, making it 5–5. The next game went to deuce then advantage for Chuck. And finally a win.

What am I doing wrong? Kevin asked himself. *Chuck isn't that good to be beating me like this.*

He glanced briefly at the top of the post at the southwest corner of the court. It was an automatic move. Charlie's wing had not healed up well enough yet for him to fly around to tennis matches to offer sage advice to a certain nephew.

Nephew? Am I still considered his nephew even if he's in the form of a pigeon? Man! What a nutty relationship!

Chuck won the next game to capture the set, 7–5.

"Charlie said that Chuck was weak in his serves and backhand shots," Kevin said to Ginnie. "It didn't look like that to me."

"You've been giving him the points," said Ginnie, speaking like an authority. "Most of his points were won on your poor returns."

"Then I'd better make sure of my returns. Right?"

"Right."

Chuck served as the second set got under way. Kevin returned it neatly. Then Chuck's stroke, a bullet drive, carried far to Kevin's right side. Kevin bolted after it, leaning far over to hit the ball just before it struck the court. The ball loped over the net, bouncing just in front of it. Chuck started after it, then stopped, knowing he could never reach it in time. Love–15.

Though tense and anxious, Kevin kept up the good start and wound up winning the game.

He went into the next one with fever pitch. *I can't go home and tell Charlie I blew this match and won't be playing Roger,* he thought. *He'd probably leave me and never come back again. I've got to win it.*

He did. He won the next one, too. Chuck

made a bid by taking two games, but that was all. The ovation, as Kevin won the set, 6–2, was no overwhelming thing. You'd think that the crowd wasn't too surprised about it.

"One more to go," Ginnie said.

"I wish you wouldn't say that!" Kevin snapped.

"Sorry," she said and lowered her eyes.

Man, take it easy! It's just an old tennis game. You don't have to bite her head off.

The third set started, and it was pretty clear that both players were under stress. Their shots were landing low, striking into the net a great deal of the time. It seemed that the game would be determined by who had the most, or the least, balls striking the net first.

After a 40–40 deuce, and then advantage for Kevin, he gained the next point and took the game. Chuck won the second. Then Kevin took three in a row, making it 4–1, his favor.

Hey! Is this really me? You ought to see me now, Charlie! I'm really on!

He took it easy in the next game, reserving

his energy while Chuck burned up his. Chuck won it, but he looked too tired to play effectively in the next game, and seemed not to care in the last.

The fans exploded with a standing ovation this time as Kevin won the set, 6–2, and the right to play Roger Murphy.

His pleasure in the win, though — coupled with kind words from his proud father — lasted only until he arrived home. Something had happened while they were all at the tennis match.

Charlie was gone.

12

"Look," Kevin said, picking up a small stick and a shredded piece of gauze from the box which Charlie had occupied as his home for over a week. "He must have chewed this off."

"Think his wing was healed enough for him to fly?" Ginnie said.

"It must have been," said Mr. O'Toole. "Don't forget, Chuck Eagan had started giving Charlie first aid right after he had shot him."

"Yeah, that's right," said Ginnie, and looked at Kevin. "Well, what are we going to do? Search for him again?"

"No," Kevin answered thoughtfully. "This

time it's different. This time we know he was safe here. He went away on his own. If — if that's the way he wants it, that's the way it'll be."

He felt a lump in his throat and turned away so that no one could see the look on his face.

Darn Charlie! He could've told me that he didn't want to stay here! At least that his wing was better! I hope he gets hurt again.

Oh, no, no! Please, God, forgive me! I didn't mean that!

Mrs. O'Toole made supper — stuffed peppers with sweet sauce, tossed salad and Italian bread — which Kevin ordinarily would devour like a hungry bear. Not so this evening. He ate only enough to take the edge off his hunger.

"You can't let that pigeon worry you so that you won't eat," his mother said. "He's probably just trying out his wing."

"I think he'll come back," Ginnie said with that girlish intuition of hers. "If he was just an ordinary pigeon, maybe he . . ."

She stopped abruptly as Kevin shot her a hard look. *Careful, Gin. You say anything to Mom and Dad about Charlie's being a reincarnation of Dad's great uncle Rickard O'Toole and they'll think that we're both ready for the nut house. They might even want to get rid of Charlie — if he does come back to us — and you know we can't let that happen. So be careful of what you say. O.K.?*

"What do you mean, 'if he was just an ordinary pigeon'?" said Mr. O'Toole. "What is he if not ordinary? Lots of pigeons become pets."

"Well, I mean — you know . . ."

"I guess it's because I never had a pet before," Kevin broke in quickly. "Anyway, let's change the subject. I don't want to talk anymore about Charlie."

"I'll split a pepper with you," said Ginnie, as if that was her wish, too.

"Not me," replied Kevin. "I've had enough." He excused himself from the table and went outside.

"Hi," a voice said just as he was ready to

walk down the porch steps. It was a familiar voice. A *very* familiar voice.

Kevin looked down, goose bumps popping out on his arms. There sat Charlie on the bottom step of the porch, mouth open and puffing as if he had just flown a thousand miles.

"Charlie! Where have you been?" Kevin cried, clattering down the steps and picking Charlie up into his arms.

"Careful of that wing," cautioned Charlie. "I started to town, but I remembered I wanted to watch you play Chuck Eagan. Anything wrong in that?"

"No. But your wing couldn't have been well enough," said Kevin. "You didn't make it, did you?"

"No. But I could have."

"What happened?"

"I was perched on a tree, see, taking a rest, when some kid started throwing stones at me. One of them hit my bad wing. Fortunately, I was able to fly to another tree and out of his sight. But I was sure I'd never make it to the match, so I walked all the way back."

"Walked? Oh, Charlie!" Kevin cried, squeezing him lovingly. "You're a real nut, you are!"

"Hey, watch it, will you?" complained Charlie. "It's the same wing that I had tennis elbow with when I was a human. Guess the darn thing will give me trouble no matter who I turn out to be!"

The match with Roger Murphy started at four o'clock on Saturday. As far as Kevin was concerned it was *the* match. The Big One. The All-Important One. Roger would think he was King of the Universe if he beat Kevin.

Both the O'Toole and Murphy families, plus the usual tennis fans, were at the match. And up on the corner pole, as if it had become his regular reserved seat, sat Charlie, his wing healed and in flyable condition.

Roger won the toss and chose to serve. Although there was no wind, Kevin chose the north court. Roger's first serve, a hot, blistering drive, shot over the net and struck the court just in front of Kevin. Dumbfounded at the solid, accurate blow, Kevin was caught off balance and sliced the ball off to the right, giving Roger his first point.

Kevin felt tight as a drum as he waited for Roger to serve again. He just couldn't loosen up. This time Roger's serve went wide for a fault.

His next shot was a softer blow that Kevin returned easily. Then, after an interim of long, back-and-forth taps, Roger socked the ball hard cross-court, far out of Kevin's reach, for his second point. 30–love.

Kevin managed to score a point on a lob, but that was all he got in that game. Roger won it, game–15.

Roger continued to play in excellent form and took the next two games to make it 3–love. Then Kevin took one. But that was all he did take in that first set. Roger won it, 6–1.

13

"He's standing pretty far away from the net," Charlie said as Kevin stepped quietly toward the pole and pretended to rest there. "Try hitting the ball easier and getting it just over the net. That ought to tire him out a little, too."

The strategy worked — for a while. It was when Kevin was leading, 40–15, that it seemed to him that Roger had caught on. He got closer to the net, and then the game turned into a catastrophe. Roger's blows sent the ball in every direction he seemed to want it to go. The game went to deuce, then advantage for Roger, then a win.

"He's just having a good day — so far," said

Charlie as Kevin moved under the pole, knelt, untied and retied his shoelaces. "The way you've got him running he won't last out the next two games."

But Roger not only lasted out the next two games, he won them. Roger 3, Kevin 0.

"Work on his forehand," Charlie suggested. "I told you he's weak in that department, just like old Wally was."

If Roger was, he didn't show it. He led love–30 before the game hardly got under way.

And then Kevin began to experiment with his own strategy, just hitting the ball over the net without any fancy plays. *Sorry, Charlie. You might have been a champion, but your suggestions just aren't working out. I've got to do this my own way.*

Gradually the picture — the *game* — began to change. Kevin began to pile up points. From the expression on Roger's face he seemed to think that suddenly he was playing with somebody else. His own serves began to draw faults. His shots began to hit the net or go slicing out of bounds.

Kevin won, and won again and again. He was leading 4–3 when, after an advantage for Roger, Roger scored on a net shot, giving him the game. 4–4.

Kevin won the next game, too. But Roger crept up on him in the next and won it. 5–5.

"He's tiring, Kevie," Charlie's chest puffed out proudly as Kevin paused beside the pole. "He's tiring fast. Keep after him and you'll have him eating dust."

Charlie's observation seemed accurate. Roger lost the game. 6–5, Kevin's favor.

Make this be the last game of this set. Please make it be the last.

It was. Kevin won it on a top-spin drive to Roger's backhand side that Roger wouldn't have been able to reach with a ten-foot pole. The set went to Kevin, 7–5.

During the ten-minute intermission Kevin saw a pigeon fly over the court and swoop down toward Charlie. As it hovered near him, Ginnie said, whispering, "Charlie's got company!"

"I've noticed," Kevin whispered back. "I

wonder if it's one of his friends from the church steeple."

"Maybe one of the World War One fliers," Ginnie said.

About two minutes later the stranger flew off, finding a perch on a tree not far from the tennis court. *He's going to wait for Charlie,* Kevin thought. *Oh, well. What can you expect? Pigeons want to be with pigeons, don't they?*

The third set started. *Well, man, this is it. The last one. Who's going to win it? You or Murph? If you do, you'll make yourself and a few people — and a certain pigeon — real proud of you. If you don't, you'll blow Roger's head up so big he won't be able to put a hat on. As for Charlie, he'll be one of the most disappointed pigeons around that church steeple. It's up to you.*

It was Kevin's serve. He was nervous. His first serve, a hard-driven ball, slammed into the net for a fault. His next was good. Roger lobbed it, and Kevin returned it, making sure of one thing and one thing only — *that the ball would go over the net and stay within bounds.*

Roger played the ball well, driving it back to the empty space across the net. Kevin bolted to the spot, knocking the ball back with a clean, solid drive.

As the game went on he made no spectacular plays, nothing that anyone had reason to shout about. It was Roger who was the aggressor, hitting the ball hard, trying to wallop it out of Kevin's reach. But most of his hits resulted in errors, and they kept piling up until there were just too many. Kevin won, game–love.

He played the next game in the same easy, deliberate way. And won that, too. Then Roger changed his tack, as if he realized that his aggressiveness wasn't doing him any good. He won, game–30.

And, as if he had discovered the winning formula, he took the next one, too. Game–15.

It was tied up now, 2–2.

Roger's serve. A fault. His next was good, a hard, curving drive that sailed directly at Kevin. Kevin, trying to keep loose, swung at the ball and *missed it completely.*

His heart sank. His knees went weak. *What's happened to me? I was on top of him the first two games. Since then he's been on top of me. Where have I slipped?*

"Pull yourself together, Kevie." He heard a distinctive voice coming from the top of a pole. "Settle down. You've got the makings. I know you've got the makings."

Thanks, Charlie. But right now I don't seem to know where they are!

Roger won the game with no trouble. Roger 3; Kevin 2.

It was now the sixth game. And Kevin's turn to serve. Carefully, he stepped behind the base-line, tossed up the ball, rose on his tiptoes and drove the ball hard toward the opposite side of the court. Fault! The ball hit just outside of the sideline.

He tried again. Another fault as the ball plowed into the net. Love–15.

He lost the next point too, on a soft hit that Roger socked back at him into his backhand corner. Love–30.

Settle down. You've got the makings. I know you've got the makings, Charlie had said.

O.K., Charlie. I'll try harder. That's all I can do.

He made his serve good. And then he played the ball as safely as he knew how, without trying anything fancy. The only time he deliberately swatted it in front of, or behind, Roger was when the space was wide open.

He began to score points. He piled one on top of the other, and took the game.

It was tied up, 3–3.

Going into the seventh game Roger went into the lead as he drove one of Kevin's returns into the far corner for a point. He gained another point on a solid drive to Kevin's backhand corner. Then Kevin scored on a soft shot just over the net that Roger wasn't fast enough to reach. He scored another on a hard drive that Roger delivered over the service line, and still another on a drive Roger belted into the net. It went on like this, with Roger making errors and Kevin scoring the points — and finally winning the game.

Roger 3; Kevin 4.

Roger practically lost the next game on Kevin's cannonball serves. 3–5.

"One more to go, Kev," the familiar voice said to him.

Don't say that, Charlie! You sound like my sister, Gin!

Kevin took the first two points. Roger tied it up, then went ahead. Kevin wiped the sweat from his forehead. His legs felt like a pincushion. The racket felt as if it had gained five pounds since the set had started.

Roger served. It was a fault as the ball hit the top of the net and fell on his side.

The next serve was good. Kevin drove it back easily, only to see it fly back at him like a bullet. He let it go by for a point as it sailed past him and hit the court just outside of the baseline.

Roger 40, Kevin 40. Deuce.

Roger served. It was good. Kevin shot it back, keeping his eyes on the ball, making certain it would go over the net. *Just get over the net, ball. But stay within bounds, O.K.?*

Roger tried to spike the ball into the court.

Kevin played it cool, driving the ball back with ease and accuracy. Roger was playing hard — trying hard — to get that needed point for advantage, and then the final point to win.

Thunk! The ball curved and struck just outside of the baseline.

"Advantage Kevin!" came Ben Switzer's voice over the loudspeaker.

Both boys were sweating profusely. But it was Roger who seemed to be more tired. His first serve just cleared the net. Kevin, concentrating one hundred percent on the ball, drove it back neatly. Roger returned it, somewhat more cautiously now, and for a while they rallied the ball back and forth without a misplay.

And then Kevin hit the ball harder than any he had hit during the whole match. Like a bullet the shot streaked past Roger — and the game was over.

Kevin had won the set, and the match.

Roger came around the net, smiling weakly, and shook hands with him.

"You did it, Kev," he said. "And you did it square."

"It wasn't easy," replied Kevin.

As Roger walked away, Charlie flew down from the top of the pole, settled on Kevin's right shoulder and pecked him on the ear.

"Ouch!" cried Kevin.

"That's just my way of congratulating you," said Charlie happily. "As I told you, I knew you had the makings to beat that Murphy kid."

Kevin smiled. "I know you did, Charlie."

"Kevie, I've got some sad news for you. I'm going to leave you."

"You what?" Kevin stared at him.

"I'm going to leave you," Charlie repeated. "I just want to say it's been my pleasure, and I hope you'll play at Wimbledon someday and become a champion."

A lump formed in Kevin's throat. "Where are you going, Charlie?"

"I don't know for sure. I met a friend, you see. A female friend. She's nuts about traveling, and so am I. Well —" He pecked Kevin's ear. "Adios, Kevie!"

"Charlie!" Kevin cried as Charlie leaped off his shoulder and flew off. "I'll miss you!"

"I'll miss you, too, Kevie! Say good-bye to Ginnie for me! And watch out for tennis elbow! Hear?"

Kevin laughed. "I hear!" he shouted back, and waved as Charlie did a loop-the-loop, then flew away. In a moment he was joined by another pigeon, and together they flew off into the wild blue yonder.